A CHILD'S TREASURY of Beatrix Potter

NINE OF THE BEST-LOVED TALES OF PETER RABBIT AND HIS FRIENDS

A CHILD'S TREASURY of Beatrix Potter

NINE OF THE BEST-LOVED TALES OF PETER RABBIT AND HIS FRIENDS

WRITTEN AND ILLUSTRATED BY
BEATRIX POTTER

PORTLAND HOUSE

Copyright © 1987 by Random House Value Publishing, Inc.

This 1997 edition is published by Portland House,
a division of Random House Value Publishing, Inc.,
201 East 50th Street, New York, New York 10022

Printed and bound in the United States of America

ISBN 0-517-64601-3

8 7 6 5 4 3 2 1

Book design by Madge Schultz

Contents

Foreword

A *Child's Treasury of Beatrix Potter* is an all-new, fully illustrated collection of the best-loved stories of Beatrix Potter. In this edition you will read about the whimsical adventures of such characters as Miss Moppet, Jemima Puddle-Duck, Mr. Jeremy Fisher, Tom Kitten, Squirrel Nutkin, Benjamin Bunny, two bad mice, a fierce bad rabbit, and, of course, the most beloved of all—Peter Rabbit. These wonderful tales are complemented by Beatrix Potter's own charming watercolor illustrations that beautifully capture the world of animals in a lovable yet true-to-life fashion.

When Beatrix Potter was a young girl, she often visited the woods near her home in England in order to sketch the wildlife she found there—animals, fungi, and fossils. Illustrated letters that she wrote to children of her acquaintance led to the creation of *The Tale of Peter Rabbit,* which was privately printed in 1900 and then published for sale to the public by Warne & Company in 1902. The book was a success, and many additional stories followed. The fruit of her labors is proudly presented in this lavish volume.

The nine classic tales included in this edition were originally written for children and the clear, large type encourages easy reading. However, adults and children alike will enjoy reading these timeless favorites over and over again. Whether you are familiar with the wonderful tales of this charming author and artist or are reading her endearing animal stories for the first time, this beautifully illustrated edition will become—and remain—a special and truly cherished part of your home library.

R. A. Roselli

New York
1987

The
TALE
of
Peter Rabbit

ONCE upon a time there were four little Rabbits, and their names were—
Flopsy, Mopsy, Cotton-tail, and Peter.

They lived with their Mother in a sand-bank, underneath the root of a very big fir-tree.

"Now, my dears," said old Mrs. Rabbit one morning, "you may go into the fields or down the lane, but don't go into Mr. McGregor's garden: your Father had an accident there; he was put in a pie by Mrs. McGregor."

"Now run along, and don't get into mischief. I am going out."

Then old Mrs. Rabbit took a basket and her umbrella, and went through the wood to the baker's. She bought a loaf of brown bread and five currant buns.

Flopsy, Mopsy,
and Cotton-tail,
who were good little bunnies,
went down the lane to gather blackberries;

But Peter, who was very naughty, ran straight away
to Mr. McGregor's garden, and squeezed under the gate!

First he ate some lettuces and some French beans;
and then he ate some radishes;

And then, feeling rather sick,
he went to look
for some parsley.

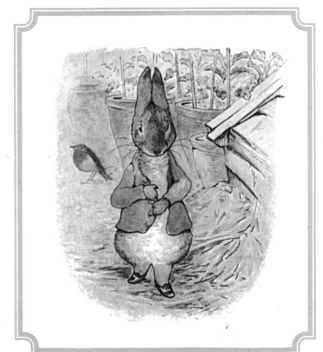

But round the end
of a cucumber frame,
whom should he meet
but Mr. McGregor!

Mr. McGregor
was on his hands
and knees planting
out young cabbages,
but he jumped up and ran after Peter,
waving a rake and calling out, "Stop thief!"

Peter was most dreadfully frightened; he rushed all over the
garden, for he had forgotten the way back to the gate.

He lost one of his shoes among the cabbages,
and the other shoe amongst the potatoes.

After losing them, he ran on four legs and went
faster, so that I think he
might have got away
altogether if he had not
unfortunately run into
a gooseberry net,
and got caught
by the large buttons
on his jacket. It was a
blue jacket with brass
buttons, quite new.

Peter gave himself up for lost, and shed big tears, but his sobs were overheard by some friendly sparrows, who flew to him in great excitement, and implored him to exert himself.

Mr. McGregor came up with a sieve, which he intended to pop upon the top of Peter; but Peter wriggled out just in time, leaving his jacket behind him.

And rushed into the toolshed, and jumped into a can. It would have been a beautiful thing to hide in, if it had not had so much water in it.

Mr. McGregor was quite sure that Peter was somewhere in the toolshed, perhaps hidden underneath a flower-pot. He began to turn them over carefully, looking under each.

Presently Peter sneezed— "Kertyschoo!" Mr. McGregor was after him in no time,

And tried to put his foot upon Peter, who jumped out of a window, upsetting three plants. The window was too small for Mr. McGregor, and he was tired of running after Peter. He went back to his work.

Peter sat down to rest; he was out of breath and trembling with fright, and he had not the least idea which way to go. Also he was very damp with sitting in that can.

After a time he began to wander about, going lippity—lippity—not very fast, and looking all around.

He found a door in a wall; but it was locked, and there was no room for a fat little rabbit to squeeze underneath.

An old mouse was running in and out over the stone doorstep, carrying peas and beans to her family in the wood. Peter asked her the way to the gate, but she had such a large pea in her mouth that she could not answer. She only shook her head at him. Peter began to cry. Then he tried to find his way straight across the garden, but he became more and more puzzled.

Presently, he came to a pond where Mr. McGregor filled his water-cans. A white cat was staring at some goldfish; she sat very, very still, but now and then the tip of her tail twitched as if it were alive. Peter thought it best to go away without speaking to her; he had heard about cats from his cousin, little Benjamin Bunny.

He went back towards the toolshed, but suddenly, quite close to him, he heard the noise of a hoe—scr-r-ritch, scratch, scratch, scritch. Peter scuttered underneath the bushes. But presently, as nothing happened, he came out, and climbed upon a wheelbarrow, and peeped over. The first thing he saw was Mr. McGregor hoeing onions. His back was turned towards Peter, and beyond him was the gate!

Peter got down very quietly off the wheelbarrow, and started running as fast as he could go, along a straight walk behind some black-currant bushes.
Mr. McGregor caught sight of him at the corner, but Peter did not care. He slipped underneath the gate, and was safe at last in the wood outside the garden.

Mr. McGregor hung up the little jacket and the shoes for a scare-crow to frighten the blackbirds.

Peter never stopped running or looked behind him till he got home to the big fir-tree. He was so tired that he flopped down upon the nice soft sand on the floor of the rabbit-hole, and shut his eyes. His mother was busy cooking; she wondered what he had done with his clothes. It was the second little jacket and pair of shoes that Peter had lost in a fortnight!

I am sorry to say that Peter was not very well during the evening. His mother put him to bed, and made some camomile tea; and she gave a dose of it to Peter! "One table-spoonful to be taken at bed-time."

But Flopsy, Mopsy, and Cotton-tail had bread and milk and blackberries, for supper.

THE END

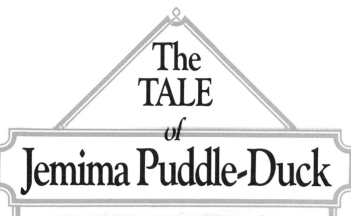

The TALE
of
Jemima Puddle-Duck

A FARMYARD TALE

FOR

RALPH

AND

BETSY

WHAT a
funny sight it
is to see a brood of
ducklings with a hen!

Listen to the story of
Jemima Puddle-Duck,
who was annoyed
because the farmer's
wife would not let
her hatch her own eggs.

Her sister-in-law, Mrs. Rebeccah Puddle-Duck, was perfectly
willing to leave the hatching to someone else—"I have not the
patience to sit on a nest for twenty-eight days; and no more have
you, Jemima. You would let them go cold; you know you would!"

"I wish to hatch my own eggs; I will hatch them all by myself,"
quacked Jemima Puddle-Duck.

She tried to hide her eggs; but they were always found and
carried off. Jemima
Puddle-Duck became
quite desperate.
She determined
to make a nest right
away from the farm.

She set off on a fine
spring afternoon along
the cart road that leads
over the hill. She was
wearing a shawl and
a poke bonnet.

When she reached the top of the hill, she saw a wood in the distance. She thought that it looked a safe quiet spot.

Jemima Puddle-Duck was not much in the habit of flying. She ran downhill a few yards flapping her shawl, and then she jumped off into the air.

She flew beautifully when she had got a good start. She skimmed along over the treetops until she saw an open place in the middle of the wood, where the trees and brushwood had been cleared.

Jemima alighted rather heavily and began to waddle about in search of a convenient dry nesting place. She rather fancied a tree stump amongst some tall foxgloves. But—seated upon the stump, she was startled to find an elegantly dressed gentleman reading a newspaper.

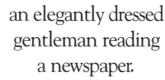

He had black prick ears and sandy colored whiskers.

"Quack?" said Jemima Puddle-Duck, with her head and her bonnet on one side— "Quack?"

≈ 17 ≈

The gentleman raised his eyes above his newspaper and
looked curiously at Jemima—
"Madam, have you lost your way?" said he.
He had a long bushy tail which he was sitting upon,
as the stump was somewhat damp.
Jemima thought him mighty civil and handsome. She
explained that she had not lost her way, but that she was
trying to find a convenient dry nesting place.

"Ah! is that so? Indeed!" said the gentleman with sandy
whiskers, looking curiously at Jemima. He folded up the
newspaper and put it in his coattail pocket.
Jemima complained of the superfluous hen.
"Indeed! How interesting! I wish I could meet
with that fowl. I would teach it to mind its own business!

"But as to a nest—there is no difficulty: I have a sackful of
feathers in my woodshed. No, my dear madam, you will be
in nobody's way. You may sit there as long as you like,"
said the bushy long-tailed gentleman.
He led the way to a very retired,
dismal-looking house amongst the foxgloves.
It was built of faggots and turf, and there were two
broken pails, one on top of another, by way of a chimney.

"This is my summer residence; you would not
find my earth—my winter house—so convenient,"
said the hospitable gentleman.

There was a tumbledown shed at the back of the house,
made of old soap boxes. The gentleman opened the door
and showed Jemima in.

The shed was almost quite full of feathers—it was almost
suffocating; but it was comfortable and very soft.

Jemima Puddle-Duck was rather surprised to find such
a vast quantity of feathers. But it was very comfortable;
and she made a nest without any trouble at all.

When she came out, the sandy-whiskered gentleman was
sitting on a log reading the newspaper—at least he had it
spread out, but he was looking over the top of it.

He was so polite that he seemed almost sorry to let Jemima
go home for the night. He promised to take great care of her
nest until she came back again next day.
He said he loved eggs and ducklings;
he should be proud to see a fine nestful in his woodshed.

Jemima Puddle-Duck came every afternoon; she laid nine eggs in the nest. They were greeny white and very large. The foxy gentleman admired them immensely. He used to turn them over and count them when Jemima was not there.

At last Jemima told him that she intended to begin to sit next day—"and I will bring a bag of corn with me, so that I need never leave my nest until the eggs are hatched. They might catch cold," said the conscientious Jemima.

"Madam, I beg you not to trouble yourself with a bag; I will provide oats. But before you commence your tedious sitting, I intend to give you a treat. Let us have a dinner party all to ourselves!
May I ask you to bring up some herbs from the farm garden to make a savory omelet? Sage and thyme, and mint and two onions, and some parsley. I will provide lard for the stuff—lard for the omelet," said the hospitable gentleman with sandy whiskers.

Jemima Puddle-Duck was a simpleton: not even the mention of sage and onions made her suspicious. She went round the farm garden nibbling off snippets of all the different sorts of herbs that are used for stuffing roast duck.

And she waddled into the kitchen
and got two onions out of the basket.
The collie dog Kep met her coming out, "What are you
doing with those onions? Where do you go every afternoon
by yourself, Jemima Puddle-Duck?"

Jemima was rather in awe of the collie;
she told him the whole story.
The collie listened, with his wise head on one side; he
grinned when she described the polite gentleman with
sandy whiskers.

He asked several questions about the wood
and about the exact position of the house and shed.
Then he went out, and trotted down the village.
He went to look for two foxhound puppies who were out at
walk with the butcher.

Jemima Puddle-Duck went up the cart road for the last
time, on a sunny afternoon. She was rather burdened with
bunches of herbs and two onions in a bag.

She flew over the wood, and alighted
opposite the house of the bushy long-tailed gentleman.

He was sitting on a log; he sniffed the air and kept glancing uneasily round the wood. When Jemima alighted he quite jumped.

"Come into the house as soon as you have looked at your eggs. Give me the herbs for the omelet. Be sharp!"

He was rather abrupt. Jemima Puddle-Duck had never heard him speak like that.

She felt surprised and uncomfortable.

While she was inside she heard pattering feet round the back of the shed. Someone with a black nose sniffed at the bottom of the door, and then locked it.

Jemima became much alarmed.

A moment afterward there were most awful noises— barking, baying, growls and howls, squealing and groans.

And nothing more was ever seen of that foxy-whiskered gentleman.

Presently Kep opened the door of
the shed and let out Jemima Puddle-Duck.

Unfortunately the puppies rushed in and
gobbled up all the eggs before he could stop them.

He had a bite on his ear,
and both the puppies were limping.

Jemima Puddle-Duck was escorted
home in tears on account of those eggs.

She laid some more in June,
and she was permitted to keep them herself:
but only four of them hatched.

Jemima Puddle-Duck said that it was because
of her nerves; but she had always been a bad sitter.

THE END

The
TALE
of
Benjamin Bunny

FOR THE CHILDREN OF
SAWREY FROM
OLD MR. BUNNY

ONE morning
a little rabbit sat
on a bank.
He pricked his ears
and listened to the
trit-trot, trit-trot
of a pony.
A gig was coming
along the road;
it was driven by
Mr. McGregor, and
beside him sat Mrs. McGregor in her best bonnet.

As soon as they had passed, little Benjamin Bunny slid down
into the road, and set off—with a hop, skip, and a jump—to call upon
his relations, who lived in the wood at the back of Mr. McGregor's garden.

That wood was full of rabbit holes; and in the neatest, sandiest hole of all
lived Benjamin's aunt and his cousins—Flopsy, Mopsy, Cotton-tail, and Peter.
Old Mrs. Rabbit was a widow; she earned her living by knitting rabbit-wool
mittens and muffatees (I once bought a pair at a bazaar).

She also sold herbs,
and rosemary tea,
and rabbit-tobacco
(which is what we
call lavender).

Little Benjamin did not
very much want to see
his Aunt. He came
round the back of the
fir tree, and nearly
tumbled upon the top
of his Cousin Peter.

Peter was sitting by himself. He looked poorly, and was dressed in a red cotton pocket-handkerchief. "Peter," said little Benjamin, in a whisper, "who has got your clothes?"

Peter replied, "The scare-crow in Mr. McGregor's garden," and described how he had been chased

about the garden, and had dropped his shoes and coat. Little Benjamin sat down beside his cousin and assured him that Mr. McGregor had gone out in a gig, and Mrs. McGregor also; and certainly for the day, because she was wearing her best bonnet.

Peter said he hoped it would rain. At this point old Mrs. Rabbit's voice was heard inside the rabbit hole, calling: "Cotton-tail! Cotton-tail! fetch some more camomile!" Peter said he thought he might feel better if he went for a walk.

They went away hand in hand, and got upon the flat top of the wall at the bottom of the wood. From here they looked down into Mr. McGregor's garden. Peter's coat and shoes were plainly to be seen upon the scarecrow, topped with an old tam-o'-shanter of Mr. McGregor's.

❧ 27 ❧

Little Benjamin said:
"It spoils people's
clothes to squeeze
under a gate; the proper
way to get in is to
climb down a pear-tree."
Peter fell down head
first; but it was of no
consequence, as the
bed below was newly
raked and quite soft.

It had been sown with lettuces.
They left a great many odd little footmarks all over
the bed, especially little Benjamin, who was wearing clogs.
Little Benjamin said that the first thing to be
done was to get back Peter's clothes, in order that they
might be able to use the pocket-handkerchief.

They took them off the scare-crow. There had been
rain during the night; there was water in the shoes,
and the coat was somewhat shrunk.

Benjamin tried on
the tam-o'-shanter, but
it was too big for him.

Then he suggested that
they should fill the
pocket-handkerchief
with onions, as a little
present for his Aunt.
Peter did not seem
to be enjoying himself;
he kept hearing noises.

Benjamin, on the contrary, was perfectly at home, and ate a lettuce leaf. He said that he was in the habit of coming to the garden with his father to get lettuces for their Sunday dinner.

(The name of little Benjamin's papa was old Mr. Benjamin Bunny.) The lettuces certainly were very fine.

Peter did not eat anything; he said he should like to go home. Presently he dropped half the onions.

Little Benjamin said that it was not possible to get back up the pear-tree with a load of vegetables. He led the way boldly towards the other end of the garden. They went along a little walk on planks, under a sunny, red brick wall.

The mice sat on their doorsteps cracking cherry-stones; they winked at Peter Rabbit and little Benjamin Bunny.

Presently Peter let the pocket-handkerchief go again.

They got amongst
flower-pots, and frames,
and tubs. Peter heard
noises worse than ever;
his eyes were as big
as lolly-pops!
He was a step or two
in front of his cousin
when he suddenly
stopped.

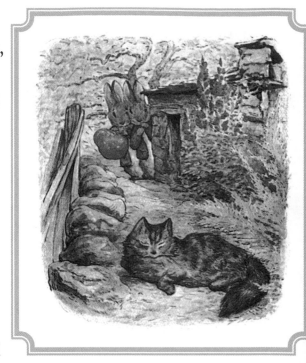

This is what
those little rabbits
saw round that corner!
Little Benjamin took one look, and then,
in half a minute less than no time, he hid himself
and Peter and the onions underneath a large basket. . . .

The cat got up and stretched
herself, and came and sniffed at the basket.
Perhaps she liked the smell of onions!
Anyway, she sat down upon the top of the basket.
She sat there for *five hours.*
*   *   *   *   *
I cannot draw you

a picture of Peter and
Benjamin underneath
the basket, because
it was quite dark,
and because the smell
of onions was fearful;
it made Peter Rabbit
and little Benjamin cry.
The sun got round
behind the wood, and
it was quite late in the
afternoon; but still the
cat sat upon the basket.

At length there was a
pitter-patter, pitter-patter,
and some bits of mortar
fell from the wall above.
The cat looked up and
saw old Mr. Benjamin
Bunny prancing along
the top of the wall of
the upper terrace.

He was smoking a
pipe of rabbit-tobacco,
and had a little
switch in his hand.
He was looking for his son.

Old Mr. Bunny had no opinion whatever of cats.
He took a tremendous jump off the top of the wall on to
the top of the cat, and cuffed it off the basket, and kicked
it into the greenhouse, scratching off a handful of fur.
The cat was too much surprised to scratch back.

When old Mr. Bunny had driven the cat
into the greenhouse, he locked the door.
Then he came back
to the basket and took
out his son Benjamin
by the ears, and
whipped him with
the little switch.

Then he took out his
nephew Peter.
Then he took out the
handkerchief of onions,
and marched out of
the garden.

When Mr. McGregor returned about half an
hour later he observed several things which perplexed him.

It looked as though some person had been walking all over the
garden in a pair of clogs—only the footmarks were too ridiculously little!
Also he could not understand how the cat could have managed to
shut herself up *inside* the greenhouse, locking the door upon the *outside*.

When Peter got home his mother forgave him, because she was
so glad to see that he had found his shoes and coat. Cotton-tail
and Peter folded up the pocket-handkerchief, and old
Mrs. Rabbit strung up the onions and hung them
from the kitchen ceiling, with the bunches
of herbs and the rabbit-tobacco.

THE END

The
STORY
of
Miss Moppet

THIS is a Pussy
called Miss Moppet;
she thinks she has heard a mouse!

This is the Mouse peeping out behind
the cupboard and making fun of Miss Moppet.
He is not afraid of a kitten.

This is Miss Moppet jumping just too late;
she misses the Mouse and hits her own head.

She thinks it is a
very hard cupboard!

The Mouse
watches Miss Moppet
from the top of the cupboard.

Miss Moppet ties up her head
in a duster and sits before the fire.

The Mouse thinks she is looking very ill.
He comes sliding down the bellpull.

Miss Moppet looks worse and worse.
The Mouse comes
a little nearer.

Miss Moppet
holds her poor head in
her paws and looks at him
through a hole in the duster.
The Mouse comes *very* close.

And then all of a sudden—
Miss Moppet jumps upon the Mouse!

And because the Mouse
has teased Miss Moppet—
Miss Moppet thinks she
will tease the Mouse,
which is not at all nice
of Miss Moppet.

She ties him up in
the duster and tosses it
about like a ball.

But she forgot about that
hole in the duster; and when
she untied it—there was no Mouse!

He has wriggled out and
run away; and he is
dancing a jig on top
of the cupboard!

THE END

The
STORY
of a
Fierce Bad Rabbit

THIS is a
fierce bad Rabbit;
look at his savage whiskers and
his claws and his turned-up tail.

This is a nice gentle Rabbit.
His mother has given him a carrot.

The bad Rabbit would like some carrot.

He doesn't say "Please."
He takes it!

And he scratches
the good Rabbit very badly.

The good Rabbit creeps away
and hides in a hole. It feels sad.

This is a man with a gun.

He sees something sitting
on a bench.
He thinks it is a very
funny bird!

He comes
creeping up
behind the trees.

And then he shoots—
BANG!

This is what happens—

But this is all he finds
on the bench when he
rushes up with his gun.

The good Rabbit
peeps out of its hole . . .

. . . and it sees the bad
Rabbit tearing past—
without any tail
or whiskers!

THE END

The TALE
of
Mr. Jeremy Fisher

FOR
STEPHANIE
FROM
COUSIN B.

ONCE upon a time there was a frog called Mr. Jeremy Fisher; he lived in a little damp house amongst the buttercups at the edge of a pond.

The water was all slippy-sloppy in the larder and in the back passage. But Mr. Jeremy liked getting his feet wet; nobody ever scolded him, and he never caught a cold!

He was quite pleased when he looked out and saw large drops of rain, splashing in the pond—

"I will get some worms and go fishing and catch a dish of minnows for my dinner," said Mr. Jeremy Fisher. "If I catch more than five fish, I will invite my friends Mr. Alderman Ptolemy Tortoise and Sir Isaac Newton. The Alderman, however, eats salad."

Mr. Jeremy put on a mackintosh, and a pair of shiny galoshes; he took his rod and basket, and set off with enormous hops to the place where he kept his boat.

The boat was round and green, and very like the other lily-leaves. It was tied to a water-plant in the middle of the pond.

Mr. Jeremy took a reed pole, and pushed the boat out into open water. "I know a good place for minnows," said Mr. Jeremy Fisher. Mr. Jeremy stuck his pole into the mud and fastened the boat to it.

Then he settled himself cross-legged and arranged his fishing tackle. He had the dearest little red float.

His rod was a tough stalk of grass, his line was a fine long white horse-hair, and he tied a little wriggling worm at the end.

The rain trickled down his back, and for nearly an hour he stared at the float. "This is getting tiresome, I think I should like some lunch," said Mr. Jeremy Fisher.

He punted back again amongst the water-plants, and took some lunch out of his basket. "I will eat a butterfly sandwich, and wait till the shower is over," said Mr. Jeremy Fisher.

A great big water-beetle came underneath the lily leaf and tweaked the toe of one of his galoshes.

Mr. Jeremy crossed his legs up shorter, out of reach, and went on eating his sandwich.

Once or twice something moved about with a rustle and a splash amongst the rushes at the side of the pond.

"I trust that is not a rat," said Mr. Jeremy Fisher; "I think I had better get away from here."

Mr. Jeremy shoved
the boat out again
a little way, and
dropped in the bait.
There was a bite
almost directly;
the float gave a
tremendous bobbit!

"A minnow! a minnow! I have him by the nose!"
cried Mr. Jeremy Fisher, jerking up his rod.

But what a horrible surprise! Instead of a
smooth fat minnow, Mr. Jeremy landed little
Jack Sharp, the stickleback, covered with spines!

The stickleback floundered about the boat,
pricking and snapping until he
was quite out of breath.
Then he jumped back
into the water.

And a shoal of
other little fishes put
their heads out,
and laughed at
Mr. Jeremy Fisher.

And while
Mr. Jeremy
sat disconsolately
on the edge of
his boat—sucking
his sore fingers and
peering down into
the water—a *much*
worse thing happened;
a really *frightful* thing it would have been,
if Mr. Jeremy had not been wearing a mackintosh!

A great big enormous trout came up—ker-pflop-p-p-p! with
a splash—and it seized Mr. Jeremy with a snap, "Ow! Ow! Ow!"—
and then it turned and dived down to the bottom of the pond!

But the trout was so displeased with the taste of the mackintosh,
that in less than half a minute it spat him out again; and the only
thing it swallowed was Mr. Jeremy's galoshes.

Mr. Jeremy bounced
up to the surface of
the water, like a cork
and the bubbles out
of a soda water bottle;
and he swam with all
his might to the edge
of the pond.

He scrambled
out on the first bank
he came to, and he hopped home
across the meadow with his mackintosh all in tatters.

"What a mercy that was not a pike!" said Mr. Jeremy Fisher.
"I have lost my rod and basket; but it does not much matter,
for I am sure I should never have dared to go fishing again!"

He put some sticking plaster on his fingers, and his
friends both came to dinner. He could not offer them fish,
but he had something else in his larder.

Sir Isaac Newton
wore his black and
gold waistcoat.

And Mr. Alderman
Ptolemy Tortoise brought
a salad with him in a string bag.

And instead of a nice dish of minnows they
had a roasted grasshopper with lady-bird sauce,
which frogs consider a beautiful treat;
but *I* think it must have been nasty!

THE END

The
TALE
of
Squirrel Nutkin

A STORY FOR

NORAH

THIS is a Tale about a tail— a tail that belonged to a little red squirrel, and his name was Nutkin. He had a brother called Twinkleberry, and a great many cousins: they lived in a wood at the edge of a lake.

In the middle of the lake there is an island covered with trees and nut bushes; and amongst those trees stands a hollow oak-tree, which is the house of an owl who is called Old Brown.

One autumn when the nuts were ripe, and the leaves on the hazel bushes were golden and green—Nutkin and Twinkleberry and all the other little squirrels came out of the wood, and down to the edge of the lake.

They made little rafts out of twigs, and they paddled away over the water to Owl Island to gather nuts.

Each squirrel had a little sack and a large oar, and spread out his tail for a sail.

They also took with them an offering of three fat mice as a present for Old Brown, and put them down upon his door-step.

Then Twinkleberry and the other little squirrels each made a low bow, and said politely— "Old Mr. Brown, will you favour us with permission to gather nuts upon your island?"
But Nutkin was excessively impertinent in his manners. He bobbed up and down like a little red *cherry,* singing—

"Riddle me, riddle me, rot-tot-tote!
A little wee man, in a red red coat!
A staff in his hand, and a stone in his throat;
If you'll tell me this riddle, I'll give you a groat."

Now this riddle is as old as the hills;
Mr. Brown paid no attention whatever to Nutkin.
He shut his eyes obstinately and went to sleep.

The squirrels filled their little sacks with nuts,
and sailed away home in the evening.

But next morning they all came back again to Owl Island; and Twinkleberry and the others brought a fine fat mole, and laid it on the stone in front of Old Brown's doorway, and said—"Mr. Brown, will you favour us with your gracious permission to gather some more nuts?"

❧ 55 ❧

But Nutkin, who had no respect,
began to dance up and down, tickling old
Mr. Brown with a *nettle* and singing—

"Old Mr. B! Riddle-me-ree!
Hitty Pitty within the wall,
Hitty Pitty without the wall;
If you touch Hitty Pitty,
Hitty Pitty will bite you!"

Mr. Brown woke up suddenly
and carried the mole into his house.

He shut the door in Nutkin's face. Presently a
little thread of blue *smoke* from a wood fire came
up from the top of the tree, and Nutkin peeped
through the key-hole and sang—

"A house full, a hole full!
And you cannot gather a bowl-full!"

The squirrels searched for nuts all
over the island and filled their little sacks.
But Nutkin gathered oak-apples—
yellow and scarlet—and sat upon a beech-stump playing
marbles, and watching the door of old Mr. Brown.

On the third day the squirrels got up
very early and went fishing; they caught seven
fat minnows as a present for Old Brown.
They paddled over the lake and landed
under a crooked chestnut tree on Owl Island.

Twinkleberry and six other little
squirrels each carried a fat minnow;
but Nutkin, who had no nice manners,
brought no present at all. He ran in front, singing—

"The man in the wilderness said to me,
'How many strawberries grow in the sea?'
I answered him as I thought good—
'As many red herrings as grow in the wood.'"

But old Mr. Brown took no interest in riddles—
not even when the answer was provided for him.

On the fourth day the squirrels brought
a present of six fat beetles, which were as good
as plums in *plum-pudding* for Old Brown.
Each beetle was wrapped up carefully in a dockleaf,
fastened with a pine-needle-pin.

But Nutkin sang as rudely as ever—

"Old Mr. B! riddle-me-ree!
Flour of England, fruit of Spain,
Met together in a shower of rain;
Put in a bag tied round with a string,
If you'll tell me this riddle, I'll give you a ring!"

Which was ridiculous of Nutkin, because
he had not got any ring to give to Old Brown.
The other squirrels hunted up and down the nut bushes;
but Nutkin gathered robin's pin-cushions off a briar bush,
and stuck them full of pine-needle-pins.

On the fifth day the squirrels brought a present of wild
honey; it was so sweet and sticky that they licked their
fingers as they put it down upon the stone. They had stolen
it out of a bumble *bees'* nest on the tippity top of the hill.
But Nutkin skipped up and down, singing—

"Hum-a-bum! buzz! buzz! Hum-a-bum buzz!
As I went over Tipple-tine
I met a flock of bonny swine;
Some yellow-nacked, some yellow backed!
They were the very bonniest swine
That e'er went over Tipple-tine."

Old Mr. Brown turned up his eyes in
disgust at the impertinence of Nutkin.
But he ate up the honey!

The squirrels filled their little sacks with nuts.
But Nutkin sat upon a big flat rock, and
played ninepins with a crab apple and green fir-cones.

On the sixth day, which was Saturday,
the squirrels came again for the last time;
they brought a new-laid *egg* in a little rush basket
as a last parting present for Old Brown.

But Nutkin ran in front
laughing, and shouting—

"Humpty Dumpty lies in the beck,
With a white counterpane round his neck,
Forty doctors and forty wrights,
Cannot put Humpty Dumpty to rights!"

Now old Mr. Brown took an interest in eggs;
he opened one eye and shut it again.
But still he did not speak.

Nutkin became more and more impertinent—

"Old Mr. B! Old Mr. B!
Hickamore, Hackamore, on the King's kitchen door;
All the King's horses and all the King's men,
Couldn't drive Hickamore, Hackamore,
Off the King's kitchen door!"

Nutkin danced up and down like a *sunbeam*;
but still Old Brown said nothing at all.

Nutkin began again—

"Arthur O'Bower has broken his band,
He comes roaring up the land!
The King of Scots with all his power,
Cannot turn Arthur of the Bower!"

Nutkin made a whirring noise to sound
like the *wind*, and he took a running jump
right onto the head of Old Brown! . . .

Then all at once there was
a flutterment and a scufflement
and a loud "Squeak!"
The other squirrels
scuttered away into the bushes.

When they came back very cautiously,
peeping round the tree—there was Old Brown
sitting on his door-step, quite still,
with his eyes closed, as if nothing had happened.

But Nutkin was in his waistcoat pocket!
This looks like the end of the story; but it isn't.

Old Brown carried Nutkin into his house,
and held him up by the tail, intending to skin him;
but Nutkin pulled so very hard that his tail broke
in two, and he dashed up the staircase,
and escaped out of the attic window.

And to this day, if you meet Nutkin up a tree
and ask him a riddle, he will throw sticks at you,
and stamp his feet and scold, and shout—

"Cuck-cuck-cuck-cur-r-r-cuck-k!"

THE END

The
TALE
of
Two Bad Mice

FOR

W. M. L. W.
THE LITTLE GIRL WHO
HAD THE DOLL'S
HOUSE

ONCE upon a time there was a very beautiful doll's-house; it was red brick with white windows, and it had real muslin curtains and a front door and a chimney.

It belonged to two Dolls called Lucinda and Jane; at least it belonged to Lucinda, but she never ordered meals. Jane was the Cook; but she never did any cooking, because the dinner had been bought ready-made, in a box full of shavings.

There were two red lobsters and a ham, a fish, a pudding, and some pears and oranges. They would not come off the plates, but they were extremely beautiful.

One morning Lucinda and Jane had gone out for a drive in the doll's perambulator. There was no one in the nursery, and it was very quiet. Presently there was a little scuffling, scratching noise in a corner near the fireplace, where there was a hole under the skirting-board.

Tom Thumb
put out his head for
a moment, and then
popped it in again.
Tom Thumb
was a mouse.

A minute afterwards,
Hunca Munca, his
wife, put her head out,
too; and when she
saw that there was no
one in the nursery,
she ventured out
on the oilcloth under the coal-box.
The doll's-house stood at the other side of the fireplace.
Tom Thumb and Hunca Munca went cautiously across
the hearthrug. They pushed the front door—it was not fast.

Tom Thumb and Hunca Munca went upstairs and peeped
into the dining-room. Then they squeaked with joy!
Such a lovely dinner was laid out upon the table!
There were tin spoons, and lead knives and forks,
and two dolly-chairs—all *so* convenient!

Tom Thumb set to
work at once to carve
the ham. It was a
beautiful shiny yellow,
streaked with red.
The knife crumpled up
and hurt him; he put
his finger in his mouth.
"It is not boiled
enough; it is hard.
You have a try,
Hunca Munca."

Hunca Munca stood up in her chair,
and chopped at the ham with another lead knife.
"It's as hard as the hams at
the cheesemonger's," said Hunca Munca.
The ham broke off the plate
with a jerk, and rolled under the table.

"Let it alone," said Tom Thumb;
"give me some fish, Hunca Munca!"
Hunca Munca tried every tin spoon
in turn; the fish was glued to the dish.

Then Tom Thumb lost his temper.
He put the ham in the middle of the floor,
and hit it with the tongs and with the shovel—
bang, bang, smash, smash!
The ham flew all into pieces,
for underneath the shiny paint
it was made of nothing but plaster!

Then there was no end to the rage and
disappointment of Tom Thumb and Hunca Munca.
They broke up the pudding, the lobsters,
the pears and the oranges.

As the fish would not come off the plate,
they put it into the red-hot crinkly paper fire in the kitchen;
but it would not burn either.

Tom Thumb went up the kitchen chimney
and looked out at the top—there was no soot.

While Tom Thumb was up the chimney,
Hunca Munca had another disappointment.
She found some tiny canisters upon the dresser, labelled—

Rice—Coffee—Sago—
but when she turned them upside down,
there was nothing inside except red and blue beads.

Then those mice set to work
to do all the mischief they could—
especially Tom Thumb! He took Jane's
clothes out of the chest of drawers in her bedroom,
and he threw them out of the top floor window.

But Hunca Munca had a frugal mind.
After pulling half the feathers out of Lucinda's bolster,
she remembered that she herself
was in want of a feather bed.

With Tom Thumb's assistance
she carried the bolster downstairs,
and across the hearth-rug. It was difficult to
squeeze the bolster into the mouse-hole;
but they managed it somehow.

Then Hunca Munca went back
and fetched a chair, a book-case,
a bird-cage, and several
small odds and ends.

The book-case and
the bird-cage refused to go
into the mouse-hole.
Hunca Munca left
them behind the coal-box,
and went to fetch a cradle.

Hunca Munca was just returning
with another chair, when suddenly there was
a noise of talking outside upon the landing.
The mice rushed back to their hole,
and the dolls came into the nursery.

What a sight met
the eyes of Jane and Lucinda!
Lucinda sat upon the upset
kitchen stove and stared;
and Jane leant against the
kitchen dresser and smiled—
but neither of them
made any remark.

The book-case and
the bird-cage were rescued
from under the coal-box—
but Hunca Munca
has got the cradle, and
some of Lucinda's clothes.

She also has some
useful pots and pans,
and several other things.

The little girl that the
doll's-house belonged to, said,—
"I will get a doll dressed like a policeman!"

But the nurse said,—
"I will set a mouse-trap!"

So that is the story
of the two Bad Mice,—
but they were not so
very very naughty after all,
because Tom Thumb paid
for everything he broke.

He found a crooked sixpence under
the hearth-rug; and upon Christmas Eve,
he and Hunca Munca stuffed it into one
of the stockings of Lucinda and Jane.

And very early every morning—
before anybody is awake—Hunca Munca
comes with her dust-pan and her broom
to sweep the Dollies' house!

THE END

The TALE of Tom Kitten

DEDICATED TO ALL
PICKLES,
—ESPECIALLY TO THOSE
THAT GET UPON MY
GARDEN WALL

ONCE upon a
time there were
three little kittens,
and their names were
Mittens, Tom Kitten, and Moppet.

They had dear little fur coats of their own;
and they tumbled about the doorstep and played in the dust.

But one day their mother—Mrs. Tabitha Twitchit—
expected friends to tea; so she fetched the kittens indoors,
to wash and dress them, before the fine company arrived.

First she scrubbed their faces
(this one is Moppet).
Then she
brushed their fur
(this one is Mittens).

Then she combed their
tails and whiskers
(this is Tom Kitten).
Tom was very naughty,
and he scratched.

Mrs. Tabitha dressed
Moppet and Mittens
in clean pinafores
and tuckers; and then she took all
sorts of elegant uncomfortable clothes out of
a chest of drawers, in order to dress up her son Thomas.

Tom Kitten was very fat, and he had grown;
several buttons burst off. His mother sewed them on again.

When the three kittens were ready, Mrs. Tabitha
unwisely turned them out into the garden, to be out of
the way while she made hot buttered toast.
"Now keep your
frocks clean, children!
You must walk
on your hind legs.
Keep away from the
dirty ash-pit, and from
Sally Henny Penny,
and from the pigsty and
the Puddle-Ducks."

Moppet and Mittens walked down the garden path unsteadily. Presently they trod upon their pinafores and fell on their noses. When they stood up there were several green smears!

"Let us climb up the rockery and sit on the garden wall," said Moppet. They turned their pinafores back to front and went up with a skip and a jump; Moppet's white tucker fell down into the road.

Tom Kitten was quite unable to jump when walking upon his hind legs in trousers. He came up the rockery by degrees, breaking the ferns and shedding buttons right and left.

He was all in pieces when he reached the top of the wall. Moppet and Mittens tried to pull him together; his hat fell off, and the rest of his buttons burst.

While they were in difficulties, there was a pit pat, paddle pat! and the three Puddle-Ducks came along the hard high road, marching one behind the other and doing the goose step— pit pat, paddle pat! pit pat, waddle pat!

They stopped and stood in a row and stared up at the kittens. They had very small eyes and looked surprised.

Then the two duck-birds, Rebeccah and Jemima Puddle-Duck, picked up the hat and tucker and put them on.

Mittens laughed so that she fell off the wall. Moppet and Tom descended after her; the pinafores and all the rest of Tom's clothes came off on the way down.

"Come! Mr. Drake Puddle-Duck," said Moppet. "Come and help us to dress him! Come and button up Tom!"

Mr. Drake
Puddle-Duck
advanced in a slow
sideways manner and
picked up the various articles.

But he put them on *himself!*
They fitted him even worse than Tom Kitten.
"It's a very fine morning!" said Mr. Drake Puddle-Duck.

And he and Jemima and Rebeccah Puddle-Duck set off
up the road, keeping step—pit pat, paddle pat!
pit pat, waddle pat!

Then Tabitha Twitchit
came down the garden
and found her kittens
on the wall with
no clothes on.

She pulled them
off the wall, smacked
them, and took them
back to the house.

"My friends will
arrive in a minute,
and you are not fit to
be seen; I am affronted," said Mrs. Tabitha Twitchit.

She sent them upstairs; and I am sorry to say she told her friends
that they were in bed with the measles—which was not true.

Quite the contrary; they were not in bed:
not in the least.

Somehow there were very extraordinary
noises overhead, which disturbed the
dignity and repose
of the tea party.

And I think that some
day I shall have to make
another, larger book,
to tell you more
about Tom Kitten!

As for the Puddle-Ducks—they went into a pond.
The clothes all came off directly, because there were no buttons.

And Mr. Drake Puddle-Duck, and Jemima and Rebeccah,
have been looking for them ever since.

THE END